Presented to

From

Date

For Elijah

Jeremiah 29:11

First Feelings

12 Stories for Toddlers

Dr. Mary Manz Simon

Copyright © 2017 by Mary Manz Simon, LLC

Published by B&H Publishing Group, Nashville, Tennessee

ISBN: 978-1-4336-4384-2

Dewey Decimal Classification: 152.4
EMOTIONS \ GOD \ EMOTIONS IN CHILDREN

Unless otherwise noted, all Scripture references are taken from the Contemporary English Version (CEV), copyright © 1995 by American Bible Society. Scriptures marked HCSB are taken from Holman Christian Standard Bible, copyright © 1999, 2000, 2002, 2003, 2009 by Holman Bible Publishers, Nashville Tennessee. All rights reserved. Scriptures marked ICB are taken from The Holy Bible, International Children's Bible® Copyright© 1986, 1988, 1999, 2015 by Tommy Nelson™, a division of Thomas Nelson. Used by permission. Scriptures marked NASB are taken from the New American Standard Bible. Copyright © 1960, 1962, 1963, 1968, 1971, 1972, 1973, 1975, 1977, 1995 by The Lockman Foundation. Scriptures marked NIRV are taken from the New International Reader's Version. Copyright © 1995, 1996, 1998, 2014 by Biblica, Inc.®. Used by permission. All rights reserved worldwide.

Printed in Hui Zhou, Guangdong, China, September 2016.

1 2 3 4 5 6   20 19 18 17

First Feelings

12 Stories for Toddlers

Dr. Mary Manz Simon

illustrations by Dorothy Stott and Penny Weber

Nashville, Tennessee

Letter to Parents

First Feelings highlights a basic life skill: coping with emotions. A young child who learns to identify his feelings and cope with them in socially acceptable and developmentally appropriate ways becomes emotionally literate. In addition, the child has a cornerstone for dealing successfully with a range of human emotions throughout life.

During the early years, a child can learn a basic truth: no one needs to be isolated when coping with feelings. Knowing that God is always with us offers a tremendous sense of security. A brief prayer repeated at the end of each story in the book emphasizes this biblical truth for people of all ages:

No matter what I'm feeling
at night or through the day,
help me, dear God, remember:
You'll listen when I pray.

A young child who learns to manage a wide variety of emotions grows up with a healthy Christian filter through which to view everyday situations. This child can be empowered to say, "I know how I feel. With God's help, I can deal with this."

Every child experiences a variety of emotions with multiple levels of intensity. What matters is how a child responds to those feelings.

This book comes from my head as an early-childhood educator and from my heart as a mother of three and grandmother of five.

I pray God will bless your child through *First Feelings*.

Dr. Mary Manz Simon

Contents

Happy

When do you feel happy?

The kitchen is a happy place
when Grandma comes to stay.
We laugh a lot and giggle too.
It makes work seem like play.

God gives so many people
who can make me smile each day
that I can celebrate this joy
and thank God when I pray.

Who makes you smile?

I'm happy with my cookie now.
Can you tell I like blue?
I added lots of sprinkles and
a little frosting too.

The Bible says, "Be generous."
That makes me feel good too.
So now guess what I'm going to do—
this cookie is for you!

When did you give a person something you made?

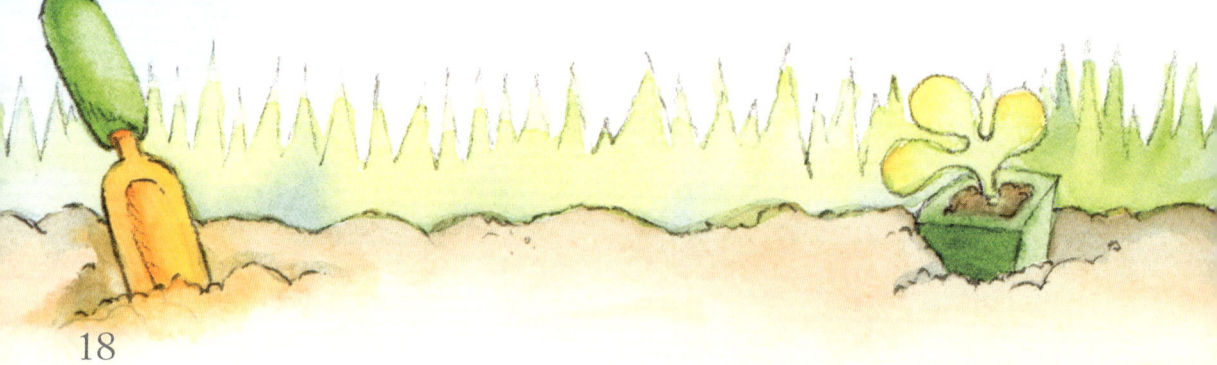

19

I know that I should fall asleep
when kitty climbs in bed.
But when her whiskers tickle me,
I only laugh instead.

But I still like my kitty here.
She purrs a quiet song.
It makes me happy just to know
she's here the whole nap long.

Where are you ticklish?

KITTY

The sheet is falling. Catch it quick!
Our tent is all undone.
I'm laughing hard, and you are too.
This is a lot of fun.

Can you count up a million smiles
then add some giggles too?
That's how I spend such happy times
and laugh the whole day through.

What do you like to play?

God gives me blessings every day,
so I know what to do.
I'll celebrate my happiness
and share His love with you!

Happiness makes you smile.
—Proverbs 15:13

29

"I want my child to be happy." That's a universal wish among moms and dads. It's obviously easier to parent a happy child than one who is angry or frustrated. Plus, researchers tell us happy children are more likely to be successful in school.

But the happy glow isn't limited by age: the happier we are, the more successful we become. In this story, you and your child read about some of the ingredients that contribute to happiness: kindness, generosity, creative expression, and being around people we love in a low-stress environment. Yet in a consumer-driven world where "things" have high value, happiness can hide.

Ways to help your child be happy:

- Teach your child to be grateful.
- Offer open-ended ways for your child to be creative.
- Point out signs of God's goodness to your child.
- Smile!

No matter what I'm feeling
at night or through the day,
help me, dear God, remember:
You'll listen when I pray.

Proud

When do you feel proud?

I wish that I could hit the ball
so it would reach the sky.
I practice, and I work so hard.
Why won't it go up high?

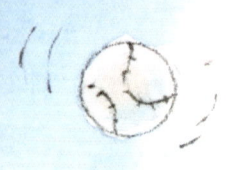

I finally just whacked the ball.
My sister cheered so loud.
I am so glad I practiced hard,
for I am feeling proud.

**Which of your friends
plays ball?**

My grandpa likes to watch me paint.
"May I see what you drew?"
I think he'll be so happy now.
"I made this just for you!"

I know that God helps me to draw
and paint so very well.
I'm proud of pictures that I make.
Just look here—can you tell?

What do you do well?

I wipe the table by myself.
My daddy taught me how.
I even catch the little crumbs.
The table's all clean now.

If I keep learning more and more,
I will be very smart.
But I know that God says it's best
when I help from my heart.

What would you like to learn to do?

My mommy will be proud of me.
I said, "How do you do?"
She did not need to tell me that.
I was polite to you.

Welcome to the party!

45

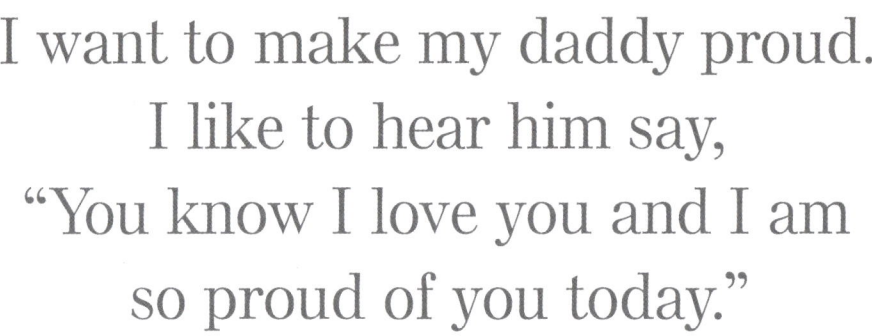

I want to make my daddy proud.
I like to hear him say,
"You know I love you and I am
so proud of you today."

**What's your favorite thing
to do at a party?**

I now can slide and sing a song.
I throw and bat a ball.
God helps me grow in many ways.
I thank God for it all.

We can each do different things.
—1 Corinthians 12:6

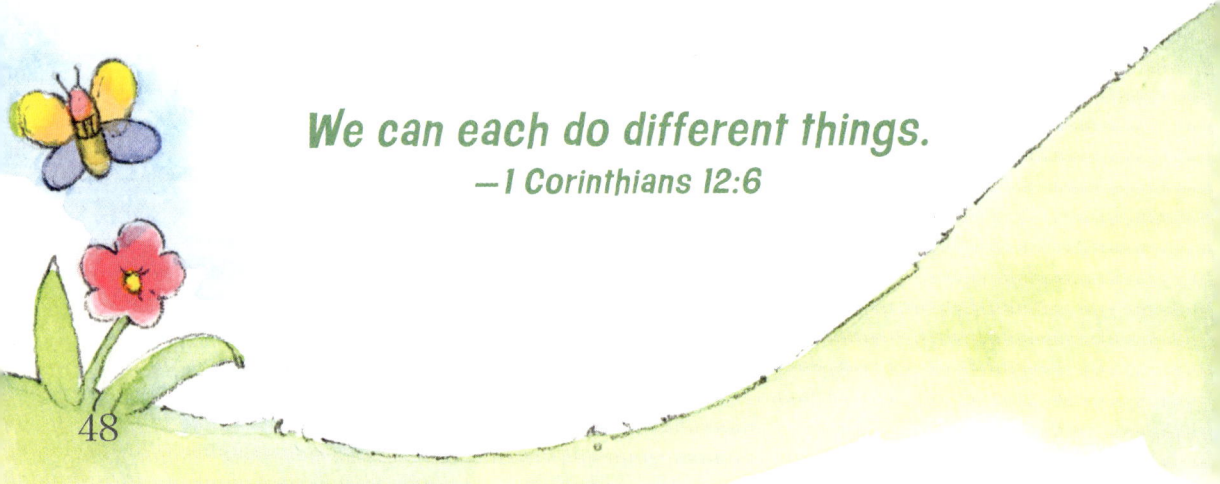

"Look at me!" Whether a child calls out from the top of a slide or before jumping into a pool, that self-focused message might appear to be the type of prideful behavior warned against in Scripture (Proverbs 11:2). However, we need to respond to a young child's call for attention with affirmation and encouragement.

A young child has a lot to learn and limited abilities. As he stretches his skills, he needs to hear repeatedly, "I love you, and I'm proud of you." What a blessing that "God works in all of us and helps us in everything we do" (1 Corinthians 12:6).

Of course, we need to draw a line between pride in God-given abilities and conceited behavior. We can help a young child feel good about what he does because of who he is, a child whom God blesses.

Help your child develop healthy pride:
- Catch your child doing good.
- Expect your child to be good.
- Repeatedly tell your child, "I love you, and I'm proud of you."

No matter what I'm feeling
at night or through the day,
help me, dear God, remember:
You'll listen when I pray.

Jealous

Do you ever feel jealous?

I really like my friend's new toy.
I think that she should share.
But she won't let me have a turn.
I don't think that is fair.

If I can't play with that new car,
I'll find another one.
I'll make a highway and garage
and still have lots of fun.

With whom do you share toys?

The baby started crying when
he woke up from his nap.
Why can't she stay in bed instead
of on my mommy's lap?

I'll cuddle next to Mommy too,
so I can sit so near.
And that's when she will whisper,
"I'm so glad that you are here."

Who loves you?

I'm too short for the waterslide
that other kids go down.
I watch them splash and have such fun.
I stand here with a frown.

Slide

61

I wish that I were bigger like
the other kids I know.
But I'm sure God has plans for me
and soon will help me grow.

What do you do at the pool?

63

I'm jealous that the girl next door
did not ask me to play
when she invited other kids
to come outside today.

65

I go to find another friend.
It's time to have some fun.
We run and swing and dig in sand
until the day is done.

Who is one of your friends?

When jealousy starts creeping up
so deep within my heart,
I pray to God and ask for help
to make a brand-new start.

God, create a clean heart for me.
—Psalm 51:10 HCSB

69

Everyone feels jealous at some time or another. Helping a child deal with the emotion can be more complicated when a child lets everyone in the vicinity loudly and visibly know how he's feeling!

In our materialistic world, children (and adults) are often tempted to feel jealous. After all, there's so much neat stuff available! A sense of competition or comparison often underlies an emotional outburst. And even during early childhood, social situations (as shown in this story) can trigger a sense of inadequacy or low self-worth. Because a young child often equates time with love, spending time with your child is one of the most effective jealousy-prevention techniques.

Help your child cope with jealousy:

- Avoid comparing children.
- Lavish your child with time and attention.
- Acknowledge and affirm your child's individual strengths.

No matter what I'm feeling
at night or through the day,
help me, dear God, remember:
You'll listen when I pray.

Mad

Do you ever feel mad?

My fav'rite shirt is in the wash.
I want to slam the door.
I stomp my feet and make a scene
right here upon the floor.

Perhaps I should go find a friend
and share why I feel mad.
My friend will listen quietly.
Then I won't feel so bad.

**Whom do you talk to
when you feel mad?**

I cannot have a bubble bath.
The bottle is all out.
That makes me feel so very mad.
I'll just stay here and pout.

Can I wash all the mad away?
I'll work to rub and scrub.
I'll make the madness disappear
and drain out of the tub.

What makes bathtime fun?

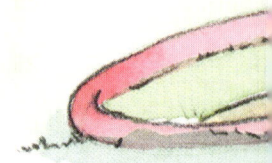

My friend is leaving for a trip.
She told me just today.
I'm feeling very, very mad.
She won't be here to play.

Perhaps I would not feel alone
if I would try to smile.
I'll go up to another child
and say, "Let's play awhile."

**What would you say
to make a friend smile?**

I'm mad because it's stormy out.
The sky is dark and gray.
The thunder booms. That makes me mad.
I can't go out to play.

When I breathe slowly in and out
and smile instead of frown,
I feel the madness go away,
and then I can calm down.

How do you get over being mad?

I get upset and very mad
when things don't go my way.
I say, "Dear God, please show me how
to have a better day."

Don't get angry. Don't be upset;
it only leads to trouble.
—Psalm 37:8 ICB

89

A young child's anger can come from deep inside. When this happens, a child might lose control because anger adds energy and fuels the emotion. He might kick, yell, throw things, or have a total meltdown. A young child's brain hasn't developed enough to allow him to stop and think about how to react to a situation.

This sense of being totally overwhelmed is called emotional flooding. It commonly happens when a child is mad. Learning to identify anger and appropriately express and understand it is a lengthy process that can begin during these early years.

Help your child learn to deal with mad feelings:

- Be proactive, staying alert to situations that commonly trigger an intense reaction.
- Realize that a young child is most likely to act out when he is hungry, tired, or thirsty.
- Communicate that you still love your child and understand what she is feeling.

No matter what I'm feeling
at night or through the day,
help me, dear God, remember:
You'll listen when I pray.

Excited

When do you
get excited?

I get very excited when
I visit at the zoo.
The elephants swing
their long trunks.
Do you laugh at them too?

I get so goofy. I pretend
to be a chimpanzee.
Watch as I'm in a jungle now
and swing from tree to tree.

What's your favorite zoo animal?

I jump right up and out of bed
and see a big surprise.
It snowed last night. It really snowed
right here before my eyes.

I'm so excited. I can't wait
to dash outside and play.
God sent the snow. "I thank You, God,
for this amazing day."

What would you do on a snowy day?

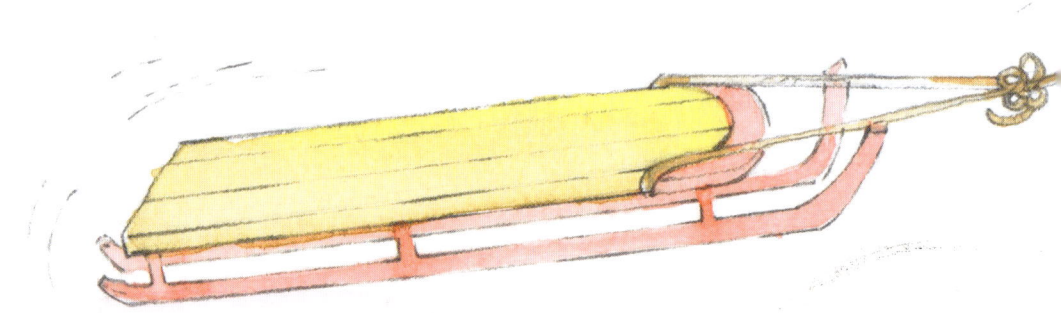

99

My daddy says I need new shoes,
so we head to the store.
I'm not excited trying shoes.
It feels just like a chore.

But Daddy said that in the mall
he'll let me have a ride.
Now I'm excited, for I see
what's going round inside!

**Which animal would you choose
to ride on a carousel?**

I'm so excited. I can't sleep.
My birthday's almost here.
Tomorrow I will wake up for
the best day of the year.

I want to laugh,
jump up and down.
Today's a special day.
My birthday's here!
My birthday's here!
It's time to shout hooray!

What's best about a birthday?

Happy Birthday!

I'm so excited. I can't count
the blessings big and small.
I know they're signs of
God's great love.
I thank Him for them all.

*I celebrate and shout
because of my LORD God.*
—Isaiah 61:10

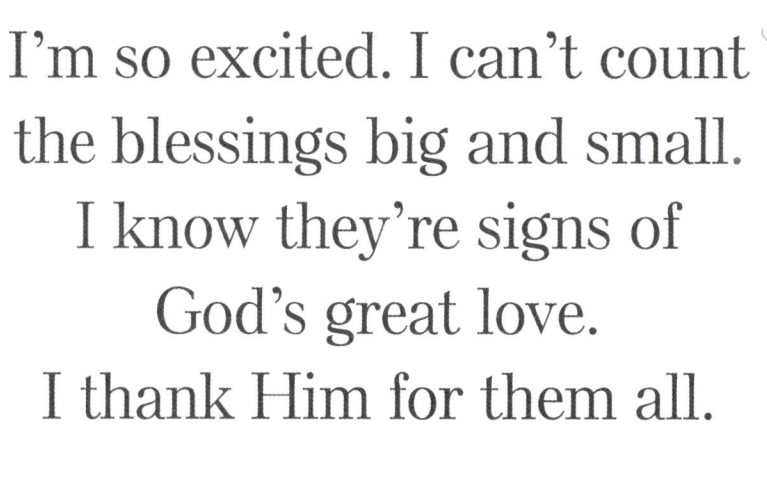

Exuberant moments happen frequently during the early years, simply because many experiences are new and explode with possibilities. A young child gets so excited that anyone nearby naturally absorbs some of that energy. The animated joy that at times consumes a child hints at the pure joy we have as believers. We celebrate with the psalmist and say, "Hallelujah! My soul, praise the LORD" (Psalm 146:1 HCSB).

Sometimes, a child's excitement overflows into out-of-bounds behavior. That's when we help a child channel that boundless energy into acceptable physical actions. As shown in this story, a child might act like a silly zoo animal or even jump up and down. (It's totally acceptable for parents to jump up and down too!)

Help a child celebrate excitement:
- Channel excitement into socially acceptable behaviors.
- Provide a physically active means of expression.
- Seek opportunities to share your child's excitement.

No matter what I'm feeling
at night or through the day,
help me, dear God, remember:
You'll listen when I pray.

Frustrated

Do you ever
feel frustrated?

This zipper's stuck. It won't go up.
It also won't go down!
I've worked and worked so very long.
I've got a great big frown.

I'm frustrated, but I'll stay calm
and look around to see
if there is someone I can ask.
I'll say, "Will you help me?"

Who often helps you?

Why won't that soccer ball go in?
I kicked it very hard.
But it keeps rolling everywhere,
across the whole backyard.

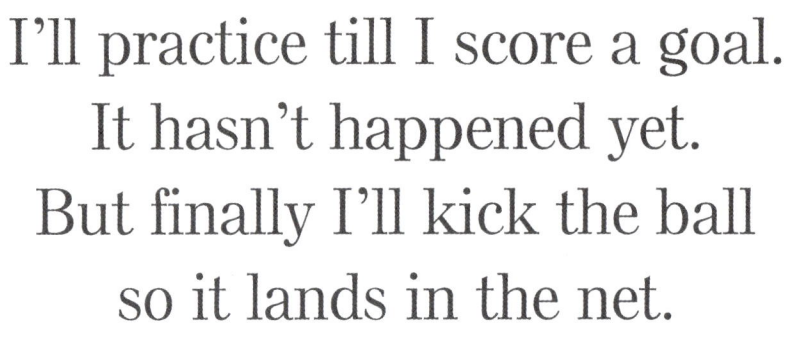

I'll practice till I score a goal.
It hasn't happened yet.
But finally I'll kick the ball
so it lands in the net.

What can you do with a ball?

119

I want to stack the blocks so tall
and build the tower high.
But when the blocks keep
falling down,
I only want to cry.

I don't want to get frustrated,
so I will take a break
and get some paper and a pen
to see what I can make.

*What do you do when
you're frustrated?*

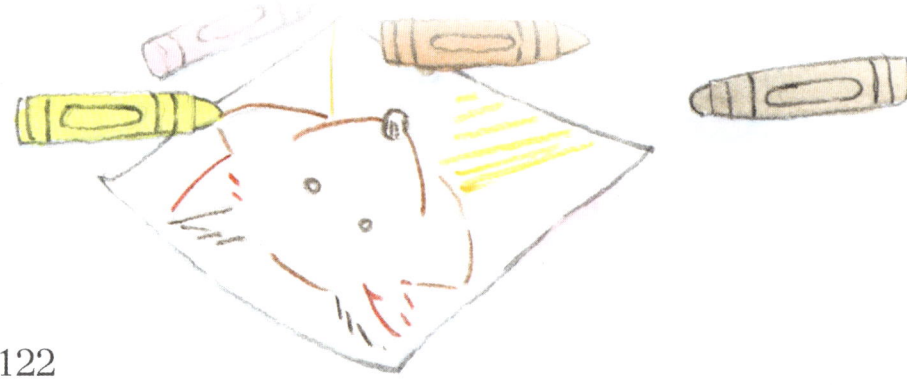

123

I watch the older kids ride past.
I want to do that too,
but I am stuck here wondering,
When can I ride like you?

124

Instead of being frustrated,
I'll watch what big kids do
so I can learn all kinds of things.
And soon I'll do them too!

**Who is an older child
you know?**

127

I know that when I'm frustrated
and feeling all uptight
that I can say, "God help me, please."
He'll help me do what's right.

Take care and be calm.
—*Isaiah 7:4 NASB*

Every young child (and every parent!) experiences a certain amount of frustration. There are simply countless things a preschooler cannot do yet and numerous things he wants. He doesn't even have the verbal skills to say, "I'm frustrated." A preschooler can identify with the words of Paul: "I don't understand why I act the way I do" (Romans 7:15).

A young child controls very few aspects of life. He doesn't determine his bedtime, his menu, or any part of his daily schedule. Adults even remind a child when to use the bathroom! Naturally, an independent-seeking preschooler wants to button his coat ("I do it") or put on his shoes (on the wrong feet) or whistle like Grandpa. But physically, he can't, at least not yet.

Ways to lower the level of frustration:

- Use humor. Silliness cuts through tension.
- Invite your child to make simple choices: "Do you want to wear the red shirt or the blue shirt?"
- Encourage your child to use words to explain how he feels.

*No matter what I'm feeling
at night or through the day,
help me, dear God, remember:
You'll listen when I pray.*

Eager

When do you feel eager?

When Mom puts on her pretty shoes,
I know just what to do.
I grab my shoes and then my coat
and say, "I'm ready too."

I do not like to stand around,
so I will count to ten.
And if we still can't leave the house,
I'll count to ten again!

Can you show how you count to ten?

135

"Hooray, my birthday's coming soon!"
I shout to everyone.
I'll open presents and eat cake.
I will have lots of fun.

137

Each day I make another X.
I do not like to wait.
It helps to use the calendar
to count down 'til the date.

Is a special day coming soon?

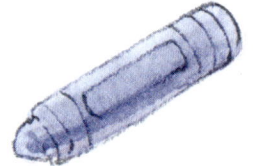

139

My tummy growls, and I complain.
I really want to eat.
I get my cup and grab my spoon
then climb up in my seat.

141

If I stay busy, minutes fly,
and now we all can eat.
God blesses us with healthy food—
I even see a treat!

What is your favorite food?

"Are we there yet?" I ask again.
"I've waited this whole day.
I want to see my cousins now
so we can run and play."

145

I cannot make a car go fast,
but I can still have fun.
I read and play a game or two
until the ride is done.

**What can you see through
a car window?**

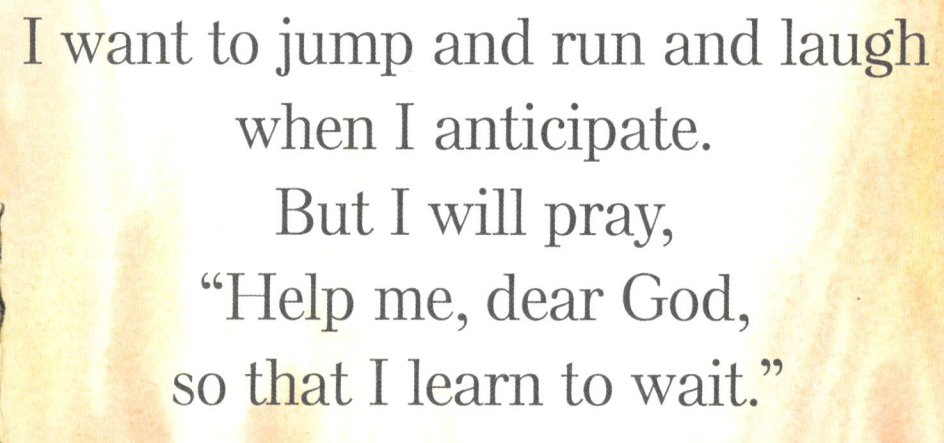

I want to jump and run and laugh
when I anticipate.
But I will pray,
"Help me, dear God,
so that I learn to wait."

You also must be patient.
—James 5:8 HCSB

A young child lives in the moment but is always eager for the next big event. Because he has not yet developed a sense of time and space, a preschooler doesn't understand the concepts of yesterday, today, and tomorrow referenced in Ecclesiastes 3. Youthful exuberance for "right now" often coincides with anticipation about what might happen in the future. That's the reason a four-year-old might ask at his July birthday party, "When is Christmas?"

Parenting a child who lives in the present while already celebrating the future makes life exciting! When all this positive energy gets bundled together, an overeager child can act out.

Help your child learn self-control:

- Model patience in everyday situations.
- Have developmentally appropriate expectations so your child experiences the satisfaction that comes with finishing a task. For example, choose puzzles with the number of pieces that match your child's skill level.
- Emphasize taking turns so your child learns to wait patiently.

*No matter what I'm feeling
at night or through the day,
help me, dear God, remember:
You'll listen when I pray.*

Afraid

Do you ever
feel afraid?

151

I want to climb the monkey bars
and go so very high,
but I am scared that I will fall
before I reach the sky.

So when I start to feel afraid,
I know it's time to stop.
And someday soon—it won't be long—
I'll climb up to the top!

Where is your favorite place to climb?

I hear a buzzing near my ear.
Could that sound be a bee?
I am so scared. I'm not safe here.
I hope it won't sting me.

BUZZZZZ

Bees like the flowers, so I'll watch
for bees that try to hide.
And when I hear a *buzz, buzz, buzz,*
that's when I'll head inside.

Can you sound like a buzzing bee?

159

A dog plays tag with a gray squirrel
as it runs up a tree.
The dog barks loud, and I am scared
that he'll chase after me.

Dogs cannot talk, and so they bark.
They whimper, and they whine.
If I'm afraid, I walk away,
and then I feel just fine.

Can you pretend to sniff like a dog?

163

At night when I lie in my bed
and slowly count some sheep,
a scary dream will wake me up,
and I cry in my sleep.

It helps to know bad dreams aren't real;
they're pictures in my head.
So I will think of happy things
before I crawl in bed.

What happy picture is in your head when you fall asleep?

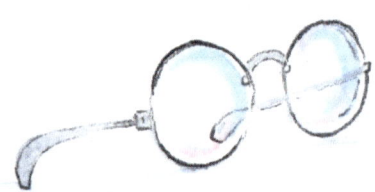

When I'm afraid and feeling scared
and wonder what to do,
I ask God to watch over me.
He cares for me and you.

Do not fear, for I am with you.
—Isaiah 41:10 HCSB

A young child who is afraid will be comforted by a physical action. When a child wakes up with a bad dream, we give a hug. Because young children communicate physically, that gesture assures them, "I'm here to help you."

Thinking happy thoughts, as suggested in this story, or visualizing a safe scene can also calm a child. Your child might be comforted by a biblical image such as angels going up and down a ladder to heaven in the story of Jacob's dream (Genesis 28:12).

Help your child cope with fear:

- Remember that toddlers are frightened of things that are unfamiliar or things they don't understand: separation, strangers, animals, and crowded, noisy places.
- Understand that preschoolers are learning to distinguish between what's real and what's not, so the monster in the closet is as real to them as a toy truck. Explain the difference. Hold up the toy and say, "This is real. A monster is just pretend."
- At all ages, focus on helping a child cope with a fear instead of trying to trace the origin. We can't always track what causes a child to be fearful.

No matter what I'm feeling
at night or through the day,
help me, dear God, remember:
You'll listen when I pray.

Worried

Do you ever worry?

On days when I feel anxious,
I worry very much
about some things that are not real
and I can't see or touch.

173

I know a monster doesn't hide
when I am in my bed.
But sometimes worries
start to creep
inside my little head.

**What do you think your
friends worry about?**

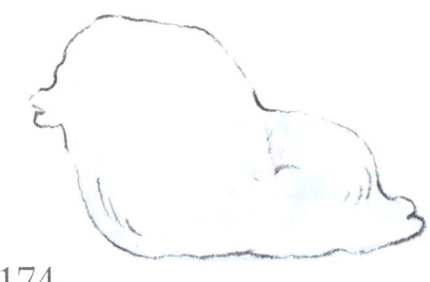

That bunny is so very tall.
I cannot reach his ear.
I wonder how he got so big
and worry he'll come near.

I know that costumes sometimes change
the way that people seem.
But I don't want to worry that
I'll see them in a dream.

**Have you ever worn
a costume?**

If I hear sirens or loud shouts
with words that sound so mad,
I'm bothered by the noise I hear
and worry I've been bad.

When worries start to fill my head
and fears start to appear,
then I tell God just how I feel,
and worries disappear.

When do you talk to God?

I worry that Mom will forget
it's time to come for me.
I want her to be here right now.
Wherever can she be?

185

I'll get a bucket and pretend
to toss my worries out.
When all those nasty feelings leave,
I'll give a happy shout!

What do you worry about?

I ask that God will help me learn
to trust Him more each day.
And as I trust, the worries will
begin to fade away.

God cares for you,
so turn all your worries
over to him.
—1 Peter 5:7

189

We worry about our children, and our children worry about us! We each worry about things that probably won't happen, situations out of our control, and how effectively we will handle the inevitable events in life. This all happens even though Paul clearly said, "Don't worry about anything" (Philippians 4:6 HCSB).

A child's worries are influenced by his or her stage of development. As shown in this story, a young child might worry about a costumed character, whereas an older child knows the bunny is merely a person who is dressed up.

As adults, we can compartmentalize or mentally stash away our worries. But young children can't do mental gymnastics. Tossing concerns into a "worry bucket," as suggested in the story, can be a developmentally appropriate coping mechanism.

Help your child cope with worry:

- Talk with your child about a specific worry to make it seem more manageable.
- Model prayer as a way to cope with worry. For example: "When I begin to worry and don't know what to do, help me, dear God, remember that I can talk to You."
- Give reminders (and a hug) that you will always help your child.

No matter what I'm feeling at night or through the day, help me, dear God, remember: You'll listen when I pray.

Safe

When do you
feel safe?

Sometimes I'm nervous and afraid
when I go some place new.
I hold on tight to Mommy's hand.
She says, "I'm here with you."

93

My furry teddy comes along.
I take him everywhere.
I tell him, "You are safe with me.
I love you, little bear."

Do you take a favorite toy with you
when you go places?

The lightning streaks and thunder booms
and rain begins to fall.
The wind blows too. I don't feel safe.
I feel so very small.

I close my eyes and hide my ears.
I cannot see or hear.
I go inside and wait until
God makes the sun appear.

**Where is a safe place
in a storm?**

I don't feel safe when big kids tease
and take my ball away.
I tell my mom, who helps me find
a better place to play.

201

I feel so safe with all my friends.
I choose so carefully
to play with people who are kind
and who are nice to me.

Who are your friends?

When I have gone to bed at night,
there's darkness all around.
Sometimes I hear a scratching noise
and wonder, *What's that sound?*

When I tell Daddy, "There's a noise
that makes a scratchy creak."
He rubs my back and sings to me,
and soon I fall asleep.

Who sometimes helps you fall asleep?

I do not like to be alone
when there are things I fear.
I feel much safer knowing then
that God is always near.

*The Lord will protect you
and keep you safe from all dangers.*
—Psalm 121:7

209

Your child was born after September 11, 2001, but he is growing up in the shadow of that tragic day. Before then, parents focused on helping a child be safe. Today, the goal is for a child to be safe and feel safe.

This attention to physical and emotional safety impacts your family every day, from teaching a child (even at a young age) how to deal with bullies to helping him find a secure place during a storm. You communicate in countless ways, "Here's what I do to help you stay safe."

Even in these unsafe times, we can join with the psalmist each night and say, "I can lie down and sleep soundly because you, LORD, will keep me safe" (Psalm 4:8).

Help your child feel safe:
- Remind him of the many actions you take to keep him safe.
- Limit exposure to images, people, and situations that might cause anxiety.
- Maintain consistent routines that provide security.

No matter what I'm feeling
at night or through the day,
help me, dear God, remember:
You'll listen when I pray.

Sad

Do you ever
feel sad?

The ocean waves creep farther in
and wash up on the sand.
I'm looking for the perfect shell
to hold inside my hand.

213

Oh, look! Here is a pretty one.
But now it broke in two.
I need to search again to find
another shell that's new.

**How do you feel
when something breaks?**

215

I was excited that my friend
was coming here to play.
But I just learned that he is sick
and won't be here today.

I'm sad that I am all alone
and don't have much to do.
But I will make a card that says,
"I really do miss you."

**Have you ever made a card
for someone who is sick?**

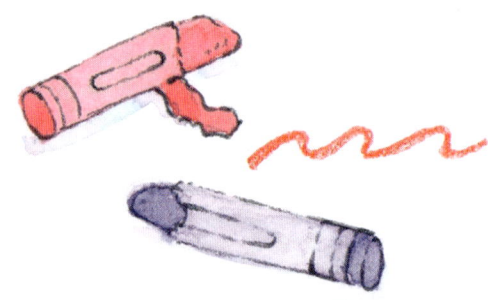

219

I just tried on my winter coat
because it's cold today.
But something's wrong. It doesn't fit.
I can't wear it this way.

221

That means I can't go out to play.
And though I am quite sad,
the small coat shows I'm growing up,
so I don't feel so bad.

How can you tell you are growing?

My grandma was here visiting,
but she left to go home.
Now when I want to talk with her,
I need to use the phone.

225

I'm sad that she lives far away
and I don't see her much.
But I will call and talk to her
so we can stay in touch.

Whom do you talk to on the phone?

227

Whenever I feel very sad,
I come to God and say,
"Please wrap Your arms around me now
so I feel love today."

Those who are sad now are happy.
—Matthew 5:4 ICB

We try so hard to make a child happy that a compassionate parent might feel like a failure if a child is unhappy. The psalmist used words like "brokenhearted" and "crushed in spirit" to convey the depth to which sadness can spiral downward (Psalm 34:18 HCSB).

Although everyone experiences sadness, a young child often needs support and encouragement to bounce back. In this story, the physical action of making a card for a sick friend became a positive coping mechanism.

In life, both little things (like a broken sea shell) or bigger things (Grandma's leaving) can trigger sad feelings for a child. Our goal as parents is to show a child he can deal with sad feelings and move forward.

Help your child cope with sadness:

- Encourage your child to think positively.
- Look for action-oriented solutions to sad situations.
- Tap into a young child's physical means of expression by prancing around the room, making up a silly dance, or shaking off sadness from the top of your head to the tip of your baby toe.

No matter what I'm feeling
at night or through the day,
help me, dear God, remember:
You'll listen when I pray.

Surprised

When are you surprised?

231

What is that green thing on my plate?
It looks just like a tree.
Although God gives us plants to eat,
they won't taste good to me.

Then Mom asks,
"Won't you take a bite?"
And I try just a bit.
So next I taste a little more.
I really do like it!

What green foods do you like?

235

This morning I was digging a
big lake deep in the mud.
And guess what I found buried
when the hole began to flood?

237

A car that I lost long ago!
I didn't know where it went.
I'm so surprised to see my car
all safe without a dent.

**When did you find something
that had been lost?**

Tonight is when the fireworks
send colors in the sky.
I am surprised. They are so loud!
I feel like I will cry.

241

I hold my ears and run inside,
but even in my room,
my little friend and I can hear
the great big boom, boom, *BOOM*.

Have you ever watched fireworks?

243

I laugh because I don't expect
the brush to tickle me.
But then the dentist smiles and says,
"Just open up and see."

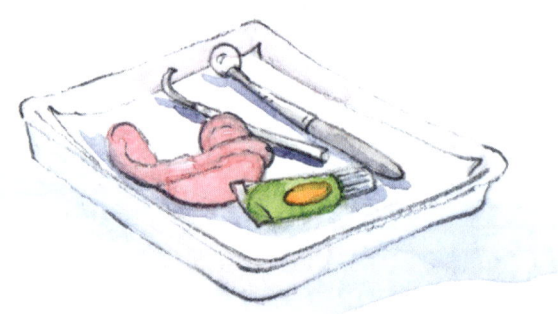

And then when my teeth sparkle,
I have such a big surprise.
I search inside a treasure chest
to pick a fancy prize.

Have you visited a dentist?

God's blessings come in many ways,
and yet I am surprised
when still another one appears
before my own two eyes!

His great love is new every morning.
—Lamentations 3:23 NIRV

249

Surprise! That single word accurately expresses some of the emotion communicated in Lamentations 3:23. We also enjoy seeing a child's delight when he opens a present or tastes an unexpected treat. But because a young child's experiences are so limited, the unknowns that accompany some surprises add an element of potential worry.

When a situation includes the threat of a negative element, like the noise of fireworks in this story, a child's response will be guided by his reading of the body language of a trusted adult. His reaction to a surprise will be shaped by listening carefully not only to the words you say but your inflections and tone as well.

Surprises can be fun, but it is the depth of trust relationships and the consistency of routines, traditions, and patterns that give a child confidence to enjoy unexpected pleasures.

Help your child savor surprises:

- In casual conversation, alert your child in advance to potentially frightening or negative elements in a surprise.
- Celebrate surprises with your child.
- Prepare for wild or exuberant responses to a surprise—young children respond physically.

No matter what I'm feeling
at night or through the day,
help me, dear God, remember:
You'll listen when I pray.

First
Memory Verses

Happy

Happiness makes you smile.
—Proverbs 15:13

Proud

We can each do different things.
—1 Corinthians 12:6

Jealous

God, create a clean heart for me.
—Psalm 51:10 HCSB

Mad

Don't get angry. Don't be upset;
it only leads to trouble.
—Psalm 37:8 ICB

Excited

I celebrate and shout because of my L<small>ORD</small> God.
—Isaiah 61:10

Frustrated

Take care and be calm.
—Isaiah 7:4 *NASB*

Eager

You also must be patient.
—James 5:8 *HCSB*

Afraid

Do not fear, for I am with you.
—Isaiah 41:10 *HCSB*

Worried

God cares for you,
so turn all your worries over to him.
—*1 Peter 5:7*

Safe

The Lᴏʀᴅ will protect you
and keep you safe from all dangers.
—*Psalm 121:7*

Sad

Those who are sad now are happy.
—*Matthew 5:4 ɪᴄʙ*

Surprised

His great love is new every morning.
—*Lamentations 3:23 ɴɪʀᴠ*

Don't Miss Other Favorites

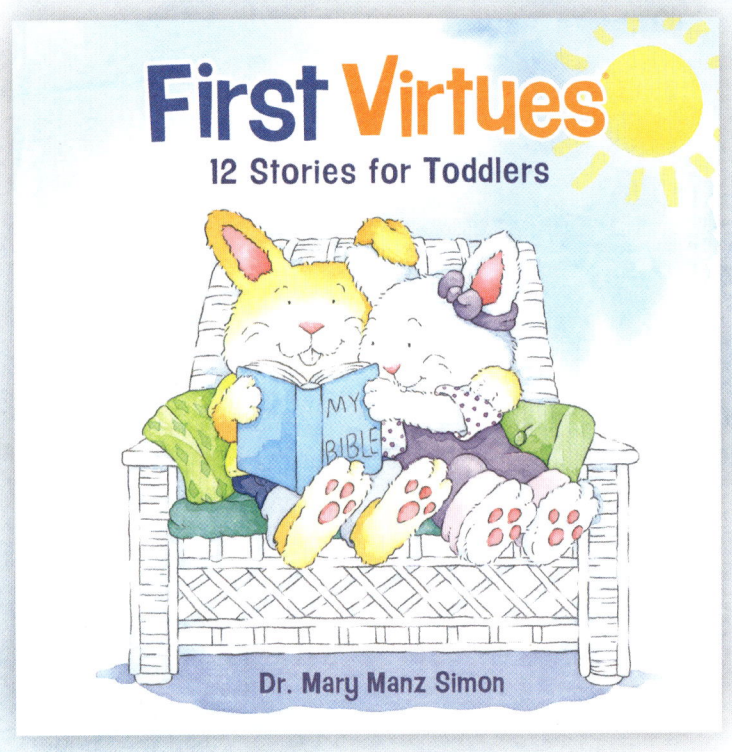

First Virtues

12 Stories for Toddlers

Dr. Mary Manz Simon

978-1-4336-8833-1

from Author Mary Manz Simon!

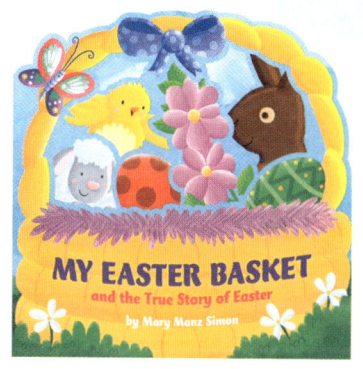

978-1-4336-8990-1

978-1-4336-9163-8

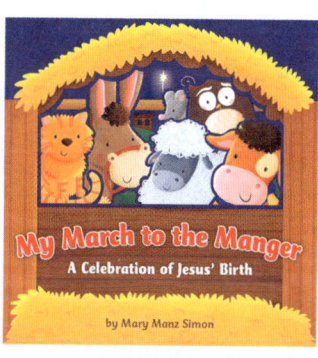

978-1-4336-4525-9

Popular Seasonal Titles